To
ANNABELLA PELICAN
from
THOMAS HIPPOPOTAMUS

NANCY PATZ

Four Winds Press   New York
Collier Macmillan Canada   Toronto
Maxwell Macmillan International Publishing Group
New York   Oxford   Singapore   Sydney

SOME OTHER BOOKS BY NANCY PATZ

Sarah Bear and Sweet Sidney

No Thumpin', No Bumpin', No Rumpus Tonight!

Printed and bound in Singapore   First American Edition   10   9   8   7   6   5   4   3   2   1

The text of this book is set in 14 point Barcelona Book. The illustrations are rendered in pencil, colored pencils, and watercolor.

Library of Congress Cataloging-in-Publication Data • Patz, Nancy. To Annabella Pelican from Thomas Hippopotamus/Nancy Patz.—1st American ed. p. cm. Summary: When his best friend, Annabella Pelican, moves far away, Thomas Hippopotamus is very upset and angry, until he recaptures the warm memories of all the things they shared.
[1. Friendship—Fiction. 2. Moving, Household—Fiction. 3. Hippopotamus—Fiction. 4. Pelicans—Fiction.]
I. Title. PZ7.P27833Fr 1991 (E)—dc20   90-30038 CIP AC   ISBN 0-02-770280-4

To my mother,

FANNY JONAS PATZ

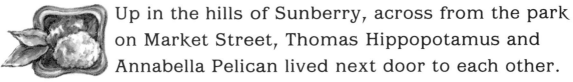 Up in the hills of Sunberry, across from the park on Market Street, Thomas Hippopotamus and Annabella Pelican lived next door to each other. They were the best of friends.

On cool spring mornings they pedaled hard up
Mountainbrook Hill—
to zoom in the breeze through the pom-pom trees
on their way to the park on Market Street.
    One day they discovered...

a big, black, weather-beaten boot with seven buckles
worn with age.

    "This is a *pirate's* boot, for sure!" Annabella declared.
"Oh, what if he comes back to get it?"

    "Let's hide it in a secret place," said Thomas.

They buried their treasure in the sunflower patch, three long jumps from Apple Tree Bridge.

"Let's keep it here forever," said Thomas.

"And we can check on it now and then," Annabella whispered.

"I'll make a map so we'll always be able to find it," said Thomas.

And Thomas drew a beautiful map—with a big black *X*
for the treasure and sunflowers all around it.

In a hole in the Old Hollow Oak the two friends carefully hid their map.

But soon they forgot all about it—for Thomas Hippopotamus and Annabella Pelican were very busy indeed!

On sunny summer days at the lily-pad pond
Thomas just soaked, while Annabella skimmed
low over the water—until she suddenly swooped
with a *swish*! in a deep, deep dive for a fish for lunch.

Once when she was swooping, she cut her wide wing on a thornberry bush, but Thomas knew just what to do.

 On nippy autumn afternoons they liked to picnic in the bandstand and eat sweet, juicy purple grapes.

Once Annabella asked, "What's your favorite thing to eat?"

"Purple grapes," said Thomas.

"That's just what *I* was thinking!" Annabella laughed.

 And in the winter, when ice was thick on the lily-pad pond, Annabella loved to leap and glide— sliding, swirling, twirling on her toes in fancy dances by the bandstand.

Once she called, "Thomas, just try it like *this*!"

And Thomas took a big breath and leaped—but then *GALUMPH*! He fell in a heap and spun till his head was dizzy.

For Thomas Hippopotamus wasn't good at swooping or sliding. He much preferred to slowly climb...

high, high on the Giant Slide
and quietly sit and look around—
just look around.

Annabella always called to him,
"You can do it—nothing to it!
Give a little push and . . .
zippity-whoosh!
Thomas Hippopotamus,
you'll be at the bottomus!"

Thomas just climbed
down the ladder, but they'd laugh
and laugh together.

The two friends laughed together
a lot—until the morning
Annabella rushed to tell Thomas . . .

she was moving away.

"Away to the beautiful Pelican Glades!" she exclaimed. "Papa says it's summer there all year long, and we'll swim in the ocean whenever we want."

Thomas Hippopotamus couldn't say a word.

But Annabella kept talking fast. "Papa says we'll be leaving soon—"

Then she stopped. "It will be strange without you! I'll miss you, Thomas," she said.

"But I thought we'd be friends forever!" cried Thomas. "Who's going to ride on the bike with me? Or laugh with me on the Giant Slide?"

"Thomas, you'll find a new friend, I know," Annabella answered softly. "And you and I will still be friends—"

But Thomas wasn't listening.

"*See if I even care!*" he roared, and he stormed up the steps and slammed the front door hard.

 Day after day Thomas just watched as the Pelicans packed their things. But when Annabella went away, the two friends waved and waved.

"Good-bye, Annabella, good-bye..." Thomas whispered, until he couldn't see her anymore.

Then suddenly, angrily, as loud as he could—louder than he'd ever shouted anything before—Thomas bellowed, "ANNABELLA PELICAN, Good-BYE!"

And he ran inside and...

curled up small
and absolutely wouldn't
come out.

    For a very long time
he wouldn't come out at all.

    Mama Hippopotamus called,
"Why don't you go to the park
to play?"

    But Thomas wouldn't go
anywhere.

She brought him a big new drawing book.

But everything he could think of to draw reminded him of Annabella Pelican. Sometimes he cried when he thought of her.

And sometimes he cried for no reason at all.

Mama Hippopotamus baked big crusty popovers and spread them with strawberry butter. But Thomas wouldn't even taste them.

Then she said, "Why don't you write Annabella a letter?"

"I'll write her a letter, all right, all right!" he hollered.

"Dear Annabella,
  I hope it's wet and nasty
in the Pelican Glades!" he wrote.
  "I hope it's rainy all the time,
and you're sorry you went away!"
  With great big letters he signed THOMAS
HIPPOPOTAMUS, and he printed on the envelope:
TO ANNABELLA PELICAN, PELICAN GLADES.
  Then *THUMP!* he sealed his letter tight.

He propped it up by the sugar bowl and looked at it—just looked at it—for a long, long time.

"If she really had liked me, she wouldn't have gone away," he sighed.

Then he whispered sadly, "We never even checked our buried treasure....

"But *she* doesn't care, I'm sure!" he muttered.

"Well, I'll just go find it myself—and I'll dig it up!

"I'm going to the park!" he shouted, and he stomped down the steps and...

hurried to the Old Hollow Oak.

He followed the map
past the bandstand—and
somehow he started
remembering....

He had a good time remembering—
and he smiled.

He followed the map
to the lily-pad pond.

"Well, look! There's *ice*
on the lily-pad pond!" he said.

And he giggled a bit,
remembering....

He followed the map
to the Giant Slide
and climbed up high
to look around....
    He had such a good time
remembering!
    Then suddenly,
just for an instant,
he thought he heard
Annabella Pelican.
    ''Give a little push and
zippity-whoosh!
Thomas Hippopotamus,
you'll be at the bottomus!''
    Thomas laughed.
He laughed so hard
that quickly, quickly...
down the slide he slipped and slid
with a *zippity-whoosh!*
and a *THUMP! bump-bump!*
at the bottom.

    He roared with surprise—
and climbed up and did it again!
    And again.
    And again and again and again!

Then he trotted on, humming to himself. And as he followed the map along, he began to get an idea.

At Apple Tree Bridge he jigged a little dance, took three long jumps, and landed in the middle of the sunflower patch.

"*Here's* that pirate's boot, all right!" he exclaimed. "Well, I'm *not* going to dig it up after all!

"I'll just write Annabella and tell her our treasure is safe. She's still my friend, of course!" he said. "She'll be glad to know—

"And I'll tell her I slid down the Giant Slide!
"And I'll tell her there's ice on the lily-pad pond!"
Thomas hid the map again and skipped the whole way
home. He crumpled up his letter...

and slowly wrote another one—a very, very long one—
to Annabella Pelican, his good friend far away.

Then Thomas Hippopotamus
ate supper—a fine fresh fish,
and a bunch of purple grapes,
and *three* big crusty popovers,
spread thick with strawberry butter.